E

W9-CLY-732

With apologies to Hans Christian Andersen, this story was inspired by the children of New York City's Gramercy House, and is dedicated to proud sissies everywhere

—H. F.

To Lily, with affection

—H. C.

ALADDIN PAPERBACKS
An imprint of Simon & Schuster Children's Publishing Division
1230 Avenue of the Americas, New York, NY 10020

Also available in a Simon & Schuster Books for Young Readers hardcover edition.
Designed by Paul Zakris
The text of this book was set in 15-point Zapf International Medium.
The illustrations were rendered in acrylic paint and colored pencil
on Arches hot press watercolor paper.
Manufactured in China

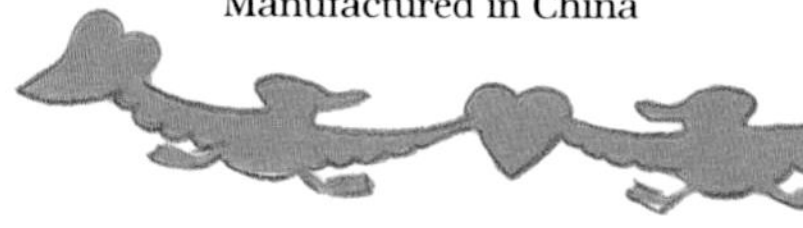

First Aladdin Paperbacks edition June 2005
4 6 8 10 9 7 5 3
The Library of Congress has cataloged the hardcover edition as follows:
Fierstein, Harvey, 1954–
The sissy duckling / by Harvey Fierstein ; illustrated by Henry Cole.
p. cm.
Summary: Elmer the duck is teased because he is different, but he proves
himself by not only surviving the winter, but also saving his papa.
ISBN 0-689-83566-3 (hc.)
[1. Ducks—Fiction. 2. Self-esteem—Fiction. 3. Sex role—Fiction.] I. Cole, Henry, 1955– II. Title.
PZ7.F479195 Si 2002 [E] 00-063540
ISBN 1-4169-0313-5 (Aladdin pbk.)

The Sissy Duckling

by
Harvey Fierstein

illustrated by
Henry Cole

Aladdin Paperbacks
New York London Toronto Sydney

Elmer was the happiest duckling in the whole forest.

He loved to build things and paint pictures and play make-believe.

He also enjoyed helping around the house and was especially fond of decorating cookies.

Yes, Elmer was one happy duckling doing all the things he loved to do.

Unfortunately, there wasn't a single other little boy duckling who liked to do ANY of the stuff that Elmer did. Not one.

They boxed while Elmer baked.

When they built forts, Elmer made sand castles.

They had a football game, and Elmer put on a puppet show.

Sometimes Elmer played with the girls, but most of the time he played alone.

"You'll never get along in the world if you don't learn to play with others," Papa Duck told his son. "It's time for you to learn baseball."

“How about I put on a halftime show instead?” offered Elmer.

Papa Duck just shook his head.

“What’s the point?” Elmer asked. “I can’t catch and I can’t throw.”

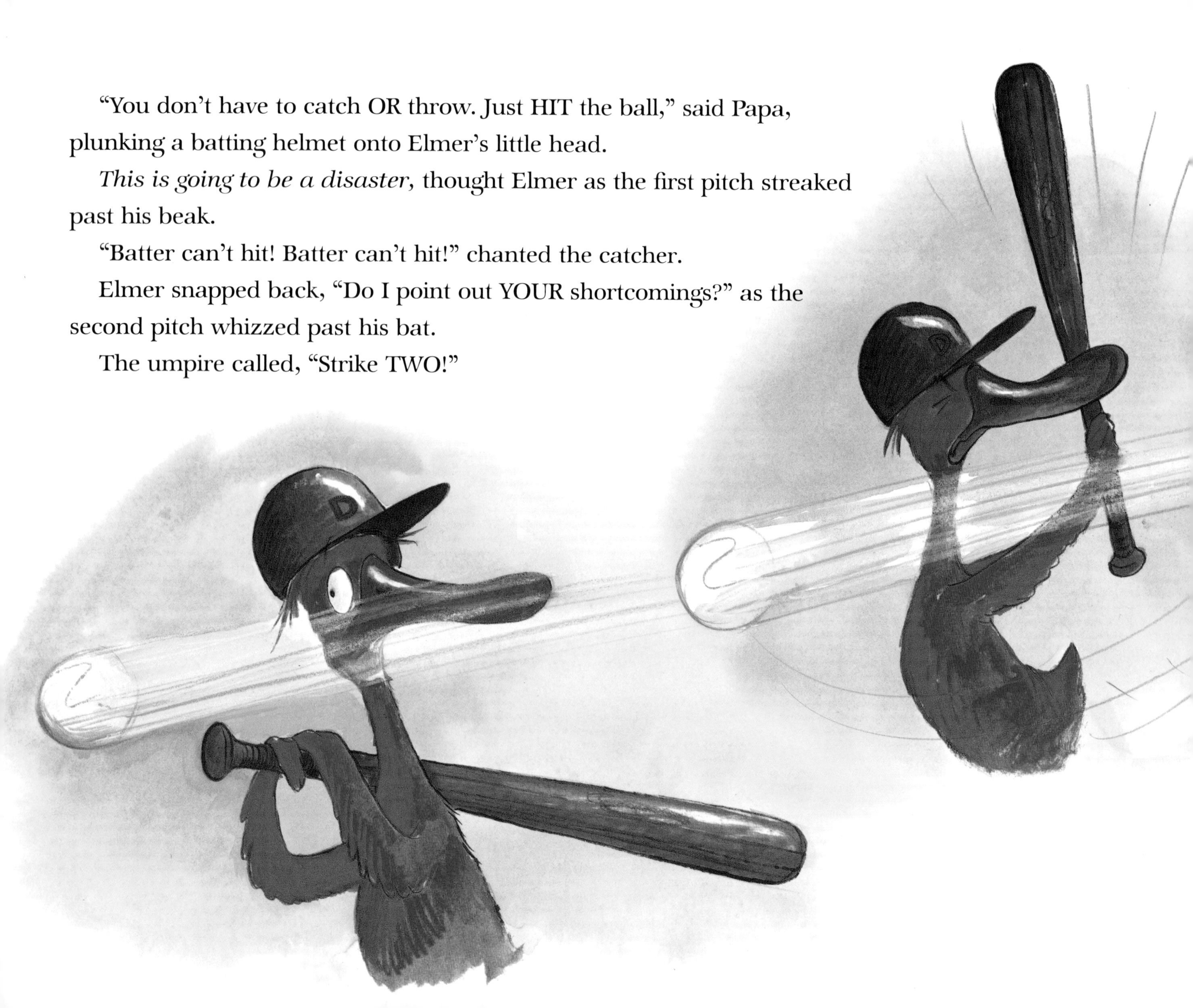

"You don't have to catch OR throw. Just HIT the ball," said Papa, plunking a batting helmet onto Elmer's little head.

This is going to be a disaster, thought Elmer as the first pitch streaked past his beak.

"Batter can't hit! Batter can't hit!" chanted the catcher.

Elmer snapped back, "Do I point out YOUR shortcomings?" as the second pitch whizzed past his bat.

The umpire called, "Strike TWO!"

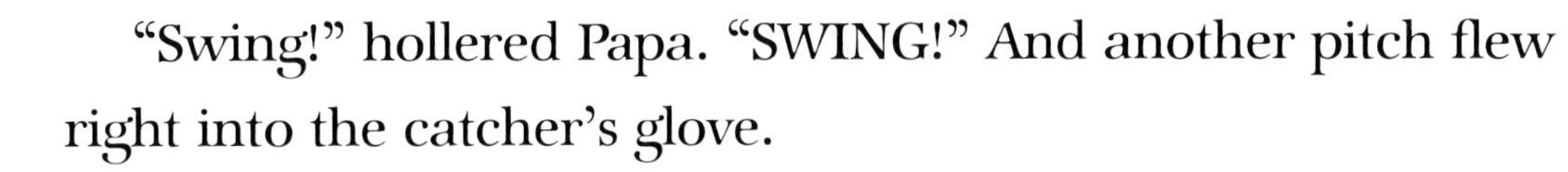

"Swing!" hollered Papa. "SWING!" And another pitch flew right into the catcher's glove.

"Strike THREE!" cried the umpire. "You're OUT!"

"Really? I'm all done?" Elmer asked, tossing aside his helmet and bat. "Thanks for a swell time, fellas," he announced. "See ya in postseason!" And then, to the amazement of all, he skipped merrily away.

Elmer was getting ready for bed when he heard his papa shouting in the living room. "Sissy! They all called him SISSY! Now I am the laughingstock of the whole flock."

When Mama came to tuck Elmer into bed, it took all of his courage to ask her, "What's a sissy?"

Mama sat down next to him and explained, "*Sissy* is a cruel way of saying that you don't do things the way others think you should."

"How do they want me to do things?"

"Just like they do!" Mama said with a smile. "You are special, Elmer, and being special sometimes scares those who are not."

"I don't want to be special," Elmer quietly confessed.

"But you are," Mama said, holding Elmer close. "And one day you will amaze us all."

Elmer arrived at school the next morning to find big bully Drake Duckling blocking the path.

"No sissies allowed in MY school," Drake squawked.

Elmer faced him down, bill to bill. "You are just angry because I do things differently. But one day I will amaze you all!"

"Who fed you that line?" Drake chuckled.

Elmer bellowed back, "My mama!"

"What a sissy!" Drake howled, and the other ducklings joined in teasing Elmer until Mrs. Hennypecker appeared at the door.

"I heard that," announced their teacher. "And you'll ALL stay after class until you learn to get along."

The ducklings grumbled and mumbled and waddled into the old schoolhouse.

Because everyone blamed Elmer for having to stay late, he decided it would be wise to let them leave school first. He took a good look around before stepping out from behind the door.

"Alone at last!" he said to himself and started down the path. "See? There's nothing to worry about."

"Wanna bet?" came the thundering reply.

Drake sprang from his hiding place, his fists raised for a fight.

Elmer had no time to think. He made a break toward home, running harder than he'd ever run before, with Drake chasing his every step.

They jumped over fallen trees, splashed through puddles, crashed through branches, and leaped across a stream. Elmer was so frightened that he couldn't catch his breath. Not when he reached his house. Not when he got to his room. Not even when he locked the door and hid under his bed. Even then, alone in the dark, there was no peace for Elmer.

"He ran away instead of fighting," Papa bellowed.

"He was being chased," Mama argued back.

"In a few weeks we will all fly south for the winter. It will be every duck for himself. Only the strong will survive."

"If you'd stop thinking like a sneaker commercial, you'd see that Elmer is just as strong as any other duckling."

"Elmer is a sissy!"

"Elmer is your son!" Mama pleaded.

"He's no son of mine!" declared Papa.

Poor Elmer heard his father's words, and his heart crumbled to pieces. What do you do when your own papa calls you names?

Elmer didn't want to make his mama unhappy or his papa angry anymore. He filled a pillowcase with his paints and tools and a picture of his parents. He tied up the bundle and carried it away into the night.

The forest was dark and silent. Elmer was relieved that there was no one around to see his tears when he slipped into the great pond and swam away from home.

Elmer stepped onto the opposite shore and looked around. He found an old hollow tree hidden deep in the forest. *No one will ever find me here,* he thought.

Just as Elmer had made his own toys, he now used his special talents to make his new home. He built a comfy bed and a warm fireplace and a door to protect him from the chilling winds.

"My house has EVERYTHING I could ever want," he boasted. "Everything except my mama and papa."

The grass turned white with the first frost of winter. Elmer knew he would soon be the only duck left in the forest. His heart ached to see his parents once more before they flew south.

As quietly as he could, he paddled back across the great pond and arrived just in time to see his flock readying for their journey.

"We can't go without Elmer," he heard his mama cry.

"We can't stay here," Papa replied.

"If only I knew he was all right."

Elmer whispered to himself from his hiding place, "I'm all right, Mama."

The flock took to the sky, and Elmer waved good-bye.

Just then a shot rang out, shattering the cold. Hunters leaped from behind trees, their guns blasting.

The ducks screeched in fright, struggling to fly as fast and as high as they could. Shot after shot tore through the air, and ducks fell like autumn leaves from the sky.

Elmer breathed easier when he saw most of the flock escape into the clouds. But then he realized that the hunters and their dogs would be coming. He was about to hide in the pond when he was stopped by the sound of a quiet moan.

Terrified as he was, Elmer followed the sound. He parted the tall grass, and there, to his astonishment, he found his wounded papa.

"Fly away, Elmer," Papa pleaded. "You don't see any other ducks coming back to rescue me. For once in your life can't you act like a normal duck?" he argued. "Forget me and save yourself. That's what every other duck would do."

With all his strength Elmer lifted the old duck and carried him to the safety of the pond. It may not have been what any other duck would do, but Elmer knew in his heart that it was the right thing for him to do.

Papa was completely confused when he awoke. "Where am I?" he quacked.

"Don't worry. You're with me," Elmer answered, bringing a bowl of hot mushroom soup for his papa to eat.

The old duck looked around at the wonderful home. "You did all of this by yourself?" But then he remembered what had happened. "You must leave me here and fly south. No duck has ever survived a winter in the forest. Save yourself, Son. Please."

Elmer answered calmly, “You’ve been sleeping for a long time, Papa. It’s too late to leave.” He opened the door so that Papa Duck could see the deep snow that covered the forest.

"Oh, Son, what have I done to you?"

"Don't worry, Papa," Elmer chided. "We're gonna have fun!"

And he was right. All winter long they played games and told jokes and made things and laughed and talked and got to know each other.

It was on a warm, cloudless morning that the sky exploded with the sounds of honking and flapping. Spring had come, and the ducks were returning home. They gathered in the large field to give thanks for the safe journey.

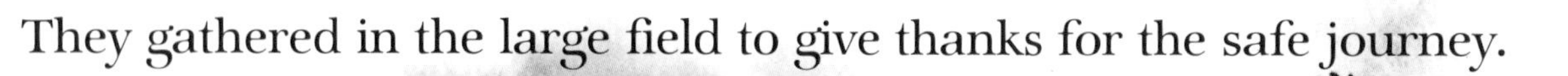

As the newly elected leader of the flock, Drake Duckling asked for a moment of silence to remember all their fellow ducks who had not made it through the winter. "And let's not forget the ones shot by the hunters last fall."

"And Elmer," Mama called out. "Don't forget, we lost my Elmer, too."

"Now, who could forget Elmer?" Drake chuckled. "That little sissy!"

The other ducks joined in the laughter until a voice boomed forth, "If Elmer is a sissy, then I wish I were a sissy too!"

Drake angrily demanded, "Who said that?"

To everyone's shock, Papa stepped forward. PAPA? It was impossible. No duck had ever survived a winter in the forest. Not one. Not ever! Never!

Mama ran to embrace Papa as the other ducks wondered, *HOW?*

Elmer was so engrossed in cooking a pot of dandelion stew that he never even knew his mama was there until she said, “Are you too grown up to give me a kiss?”

Elmer cried with joy and hugged her.

“I always knew you were special,” she whispered to him. “And now everyone else knows too. I am so proud of you!”

The entire flock cheered when Elmer stepped from his home. One by one, each duck congratulated him for his bravery and loyalty and ingenuity.

Drake Duckling sheepishly kicked the dirt with his webbed feet. He didn’t know what to say except, “Way to go, Elmer,” and he offered his wing for a high five.

Elmer took a deep breath and then spoke his mind. "I want to make one thing perfectly clear: I am the same duck I have always been. I have not changed. I am a BIG SISSY and PROUD of it!"

Drake took a step forward. "*You* haven't changed, but maybe *I* have."

Again he offered his wing, and this time Elmer slapped it hard as the flock rushed to surround their hero.

Over the years Elmer learned that he was not so very different after all. Out in the world he met lots of other ducks just like himself.

No, Elmer was not so different, but he always did remain *special.*